Echo ❧ Echo

REVERSO POEMS
about
GREEK MYTHS

Marilyn Singer · illustrated by Josée Masse

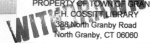
 Dial Books for Young Readers

Thanks to Steve Aronson and to all
the good folks at Penguin.

DIAL BOOKS *for* YOUNG READERS

Penguin Young Readers Group ◦ *An imprint of Penguin Random House, LLC*

375 Hudson Street, New York, New York 10014, U.S.A.

Library of Congress Cataloging-in-Publication Data

Singer, Marilyn.

[Poems. Selections]

Echo echo : reverso poems about the Greek myths / Marilyn Singer ; iIllustrated by Josée Masse.

pages cm ◦ ISBN 978-0-8037-3992-5 (hardcover)

1. Mythology, Greek—Juvenile poetry. I. Masse, Josée, illustrator. II. Title.

PS3569.I546A6 2015   811'.54—dc23   2014048809

Manufactured in China on acid-free paper

1 3 5 7 9 10 8 6 4 2

Text set in Cochin and Dalliance

The artwork for this book was created with Liquitex Acrylic

on a Strathmore 500 series bristol sheet—2-ply vellum

To my champions:
Lucia Monfried and Brenda Bowen

m.s.

To my beautiful girl, Alice,

with all my love

j.m.

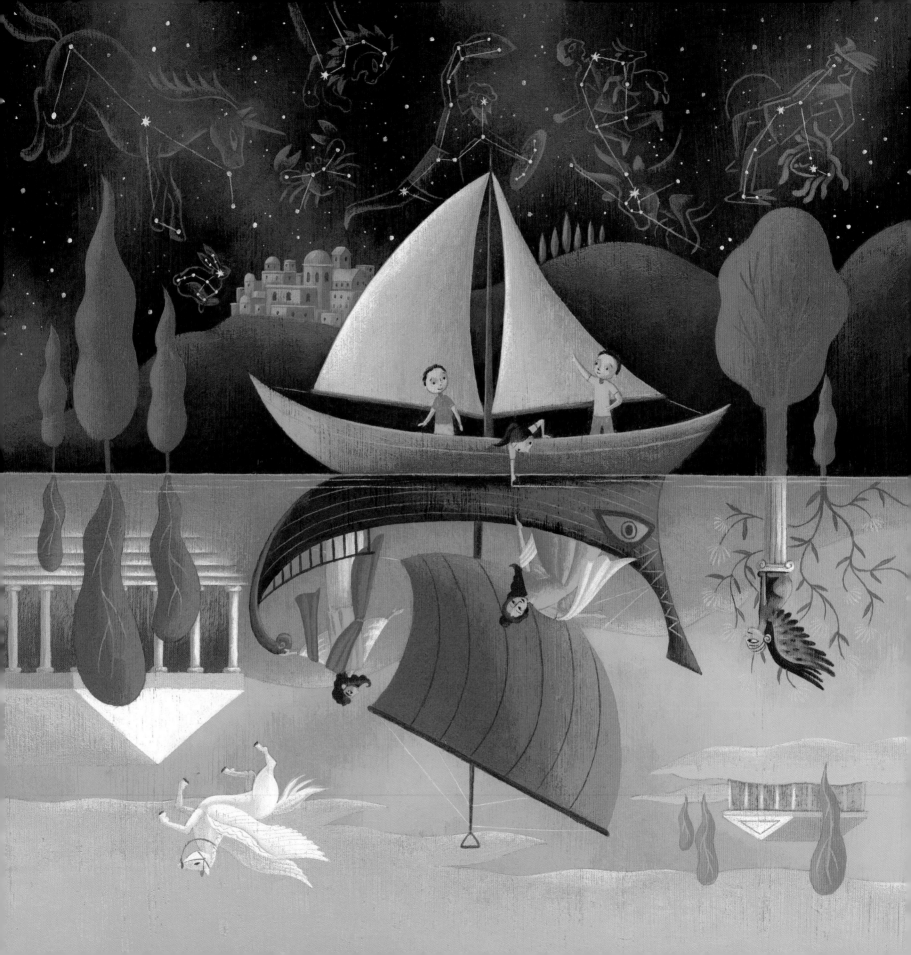

An Age of Marvelous Myths

Ancient Greece:
An age of marvelous myths,
gone, but not forgotten.
Heroes that rise and fall.
Deep winter's hardship,
summer's harvest.
Gods who bring about
chaos and order.
Echoes,
fragrant flowers,
spiders,
gold,
stone.
People turned to
these curious stories.
How else to explain
such wonders
when the world was young?

When the world was young,
such wonders!
How else to explain
these curious stories:
people turned to
stone,
gold,
spiders,
fragrant flowers,
echoes.
Chaos and order.
Gods who bring about
summer's harvest,
deep winter's hardship.
Heroes that rise and fall,
gone, but not forgotten.
An age of marvelous myths:
Ancient Greece.

Pandora and the Box

Oh, how humans are weak!
"Don't peek,"
when a god speaks.
It
isn't
hard to listen.
It might have been great Zeus's game.
No matter, that—
She gets the blame.
She didn't collect them,
but
she let loose those evils.
She just had to be curious,
that Pandora.
Blast her!
Why,
she opened that darn box,
holding on to hope
alone.

Alone,
holding on to hope,
she opened that darn box.
Why
blast her?
That Pandora,
she just had to be curious.
She let loose those evils,
but
she didn't collect them.
She gets the blame.
No matter that
it might have been great Zeus's game.
Hard to listen,
isn't
it,
when a god speaks,
"Don't peek?"
Oh, how humans are weak.

Pandora was the first woman created by the gods. Zeus gave her a box, which she was not to open, but she did, letting loose all the evils in the world. Only hope remained inside.

Arachne and Athena

Competition?
I'm really not fond of
bragging,
but that hag is constantly
overpraised.
I don't need to be
a daughter of Zeus.
I am already
the goddess of silk.
There can never be another of my ilk,
now and forever.
Let her keep trying to win at spinning,
that creature with no fingers
so nimble and clever.
Behold how she's fallen from her high position!

Behold! How she's fallen from her high position—
so nimble and clever,
that creature with no fingers.
Let her keep trying to win at spinning,
now and forever.
There can never be another of my ilk—
the goddess of silk.
I am already
a daughter of Zeus.
I don't need to be
overpraised.
But that hag is constantly
bragging.
I'm really not fond of
competition.

Arachne was a talented and proud weaver. Athena, goddess of wisdom (and weaving), challenged her to a contest. When Arachne won, Athena was so angry that she changed the girl into a spider.

King Midas and His Daughter

Golden
girl,
alas, my
good father
still dares to call me,
who
would never offer a gentle hand.
What kind of man would for years not give a caress?
I must confess
I suffer much.
Today—
so needy
so greedy—
for one magic touch.

For one magic touch—
so greedy,
so needy—
today,
I suffer much,
I must confess.
What kind of man would for years not give a caress,
would never offer a gentle hand?
Who
still dares to call me
"good father?"
Alas, my
girl!
Golden.

Because he helped out Silenus, this satyr (half-man, half-goat) granted Midas his wish—the power to change anything he touched to gold. Midas made the terrible mistake of touching his daughter.

Perseus and Medusa

There is no man who wouldn't be
scared stiff.
Petrified indeed,
I must have your head,
stone-hearted monster!
I am the chosen
one to rid the world of you nasty creatures.
It is my curse to be the
hero.
Look away.
You cannot
shield yourself from me.

Shield yourself from me?
You cannot
look away,
hero.
It is my curse to be the
one to rid the world of you nasty creatures.
I am the chosen
stone-hearted monster.
I must have your head,
petrified indeed—
scared stiff.
There is no man who wouldn't be.

Heroic Perseus was given the task of slaying the snake-headed monster, Medusa. Anyone who gazed at her turned to stone.
Perseus used his shield as a mirror so that he didn't have to look directly at her face. After he beheaded her, some of
the drops of blood turned into Pegasus, the winged horse.

Bellerophon with Pegasus

Everyone could
see that the mission was impossible.
Who could
fell
that fiery legend?
Bellerophon,
brave, arrogant!
Spurring him on
were
dreams of glory,
gods,
Olympus.
His aim was to reach, mount
the white-winged horse with the golden bridle,
riding
long and hard after the dreaded Chimera.
At that moment,
he
wasn't
expecting immortality.

Expecting immortality,
wasn't
he?
At that moment,
long and hard after the dreaded Chimera,
riding
the white-winged horse with the golden bridle,
his aim was to reach Mount
Olympus.
Gods,
dreams of glory
were
spurring him on.
Brave, arrogant
Bellerophon,
that fiery legend,
fell.
Who could
see that the mission was impossible?
Everyone could.

Like Perseus, Bellerophon also had to slay a monster—the Chimera, a fire-breathing combination of lion, goat, and serpent.
To do so, he had to ride Pegasus, after capturing the horse with a magical golden bridle. When he succeeded in his
mission, the hero believed he should be made a god. He tried to fly to Mount Olympus—and failed.

Narcissus and Echo

"Here,
here…"
Was
that
a nymph?
Was
that
an echo?
Leave me,
foolish pursuer!
I will forever be the
only
one
that
I desire—
the most beautiful of youths—
a flower among men.

A flower among men!
The most beautiful of youths!
I desire
that
one
only.
I will forever be the
foolish pursuer.
Leave me,
an echo
that
was
a nymph,
that
was
here.
"Here…"

Narcissus was a vain young man. He spurned the young woman, Echo, who loved him. She was turned into just a mournful
sound—an echo. He fell in love with his reflection in a pond, wasted away, and was transformed into a flower.

Pygmalion and Galatea

Wondrous!
How
life-
like!
There is nothing is this world
so perfect.
Oh, these lips, hands, eyes!
The artist
is in love with
his creation.
Let a heartfelt wish be granted,
kind Venus:
Only you could make this stone breathe!

Only you could make this stone breathe!
Kind Venus
let a heartfelt wish be granted.
His creation
is in love with
the artist.
Oh, these lips, hands, eyes—
so perfect!
There is nothing in this world
like
life!
How
wondrous!

The great sculptor Pygmalion carved a beautiful statue. He asked Aphrodite, the goddess of love (also called Venus), to bring him a woman like his creation. Understanding what he really wanted, she brought the statue Galatea to life. The pair married and lived happily ever after.

Theseus and Ariadne

Trust this, hero:
The way in is
easy, but
the way out of this labyrinth is not.
To escape
means
possession of the secret.
To be
a king
you must willingly offer
to help those in peril.
Hungry,
the Minotaur waits.
Courage!
Lives hang by
the slenderest thread.
Do not lose
hope.

Hope!
Do not lose
the slenderest thread
lives hang by.
Courage!
The Minotaur waits.
Hungry
to help those in peril,
you must willingly offer
a king-
to-be
possession of the secret
means
to escape.
The way out of this labyrinth is not
easy, but
the way in is.
Trust this hero.

To stop the Minoans from attacking them, every nine years the Athenians were forced to send fourteen boys and girls to the labyrinth in Minos, where they were eaten by the Minotaur, a creature half bull and half man. Theseus, who was to become king of Athens, put an end to this by killing the monster. The king's daughter, Ariadne, gave Theseus a ball of thread to help him find his way back out of the maze.

Icarus and Daedalus

Dark sea is below,
bright heaven waits above.
I feel the sun's great glow.
I hear him saying,
"By Apollo, no!
Not too high!
Take care,
my son!"
But, oh,
these precious waxen wings
so open up
the sky!
I understand
the glory of soaring.
I know
why
we burn to fly!

We burn to fly.
Why,
I know
the glory of soaring.
I understand
the sky.
So, open up
these precious waxen wings,
but, oh,
my son,
take care!
Not too high…
By Apollo, no!
I hear him saying,
"I feel the sun's great glow."
Bright heaven waits above,
dark sea is below.

When the designer of the labyrinth, Daedalus, was imprisoned there with his son, Icarus, he fashioned wings out of wax and feathers so that the pair could escape. He warned Icarus not to fly too close to the sun or the wax would melt. Icarus did not obey and plunged to his death in the sea.

FINISH

Melanion and Atalanta

Dazzling beauty!
This apple of
my eye
catches
my fancy.
Each shining movement captures
poetry in motion.
An irresistible jewel!
Oh, but I must overtake such
a wife!
I do not wish to be declared
the loser of this race,
who is bound to forfeit a happy life.

Who is bound to forfeit a happy life?
The loser of this race.
I do not wish to be declared
a wife.
Oh, but I must overtake such
an irresistible jewel.
Poetry in motion!
Each shining movement captures
my fancy,
catches
my eye—
this apple of
dazzling beauty!

Atalanta, an athlete and warrior, did not want to be a bride. Melanion (also called Hippomenes in some versions of the myth) was Atalanta's suitor, who had to beat her in a race. He threw three golden apples at her to prevent her from winning. If he'd lost, he would've been killed. But he won—and they were married.

Demeter and Persephone

I hate the thief.
Do not ask that
I forgive Hades.
Spring
will turn to
winter,
will leave this land cold and dark.
Daughter,
this mother's lonely
tears
shed no
relief.
I feel such
despair.
No more
flowers blooming, trees in leaf.
There will be
six months of grief
after
so much joy and laughter.

So much joy and laughter
after
six months of grief.
There will be
flowers blooming, trees in leaf.
No more
despair.
I feel such
relief.
Shed no
tears.
This mother's lonely
daughter
will leave this land, cold and dark.
Winter
will turn to
spring.
I forgive Hades.
Do not ask that
I hate the thief.

Hades, god of the underworld, fell in love with and kidnapped Persephone, the beautiful daughter of Demeter, goddess of the earth's bounty. Distraught Demeter searched everywhere and threatened to make earth barren if her daughter was not returned. Finally, a deal was struck. Persephone would live six months among the dead and six months among the living—and people on earth would experience the turning of the seasons every year.

Eurydice and Orpheus

In the end, the dead must stay with the dead.
There are rules that must not be broken—
however, you should know,
the music moved him so!
Weeping, the king of the unseen declared,
"Leave this world below,
and Eurydice will never
look back.
Go, but take care."
My dear Orpheus—
he told me
the path we now must follow:
pain
leading to
promise,
gray gloom
fading to
light!
A second chance at romance is what lies ahead,
not
our final farewell.

Our final farewell,
not
a second chance at romance is what lies ahead.
Light
fading to
gray gloom,
promise
leading to
pain—
the path we now must follow.
He told me,
"My dear Orpheus,
go—but take care.
Look back,
and Eurydice will never
leave this world below."
Weeping, the king of the unseen declared
the music moved him so.
However, you should know
there are rules that must not be broken.
In the end, the dead must stay with the dead.

Orpheus was a great musician. When his beloved Eurydice died, he went to the land of the dead to bring her back to life.
His music melted the heart of Hades, god of the underworld, who allowed Orpheus to take Eurydice with him—but only
if he did not look back at her until they fully reached the upper world. He did look back, and she disappeared.

Gods and Mortals

These myths
make sense of
the world.
We—
tellers and listeners alike—
enter these portals to
gods and mortals.
They can never again be closed,
once our imaginations are opened.

Once our imaginations are opened,
they can never again be closed.
Gods and mortals
enter these portals to
tellers and listeners alike.
We,
the world,
make sense of
these myths.

ABOUT THIS BOOK

Every civilization tells stories. Some are about how the world began or why we have seasons or where a flower or a river or a mountain came from. Others are about heroes facing monsters and other magical beings. Many of these tales feature gods and goddesses. We call these stories "myths."

Among the best-known myths are the ones created by the ancient Greeks. They believed in gods who lived on Mount Olympus (except for Hades, who resided in the Underworld). These deities had supernatural abilities, but human emotions. They were capable of arguing among themselves and even causing wars. On Earth (and often in disguise), they interacted with people, sometimes to the benefit of these men and women, sometimes not. Athena, goddess of wisdom, challenged Arachne to a weaving contest. Arachne won—then lost when Athena changed her into a spider. Aphrodite, goddess of love, took pity on the sculptor Pygmalion and turned his beloved statue, Galatea, into a real live girl, whom he happily married.

Greek mythology also portrayed the strengths and weaknesses of human beings, such as courage, pride, vanity, curiosity, and endurance. Pandora's curiosity made her peer into a box she'd been forbidden to open, thereby unleashing all the evils into the world. Icarus's vanity caused him to defy his father's warning and fly on his waxen wings too close to the sun.

This book features a number of these myths in the form of poems. The poems themselves are all reversos, a poetry form I invented. A reverso consists of two poems. You read the first poem top to bottom. Then,

you read the poem again with the lines reversed, with changes only in punctuation and capitalization, and that second poem says something completely different. It may be spoken by the same character at a different point in time or with a different point of view, or—in this collection—it may be spoken by another character altogether. For example, King Midas's daughter speaks of her longing for her father's kind touch, and then the king, given the gift of turning anything he touches into gold, mourns turning his beloved child into hard metal. Perseus declares that he will have snake-haired Medusa's head, while Medusa claims she will have his. The reversos are a new way of looking at old, unforgettable tales.

You can read the myths themselves in: *Mythology* by Edith Hamilton, *Bulfinch's Mythology: The Age of Fable*, and *D'Aulaires' Book of Greek Myths*. And you can read more reversos in my books *Mirror Mirror* and *Follow Follow*. I hope you will try to write your own reversos. It's challenging but so much fun.